MW01141062

12 EPIC
ANIMAL ADVENTURES

by Janet Slingerland

www.12StoryLibrary.com

12-Story Library is an imprint of Bookstaves.

Photographs ©: SeanPavonePhoto/iStockphoto, cover, 1; JJ Harrison/CC3.0, 4; TORLEY/ CC2.0, 5; Gil.K/Shutterstock.com, 6; Hp.Baumeler/CC4.0, 7; stockcam/iStockphoto, 8; stockcam/iStockphoto, 9; Max Topchii/Shutterstock.com, 10; Rosemary Calvert/ Getty Images, 11; IrinaK/Shutterstock.com, 12; irin717/iStockphoto, 13; Jo Ann Snover/ Shutterstock.com, 14; Kfulgham84/CC3.0, 15; Adam Jones/CC2.0, 16; JHVEPhoto/ iStockphoto, 17; Mosaikphotography/iStockphoto,18; Sagariha/CC4.0, 19; CrackerClips/ iStockphoto, 20; Ann Froschauer/USFWS, 21; milehightraveler/iStockphoto, 21; Jaap2/iStockphoto, 22; BlueOrange Studio/Shutterstock.com, 23; Pascale Gueret/ Shutterstock.com, 24; Alberto Loyo/Shutterstock.com, 25; davidkl/iStockphoto, 26; ChuckSchugPhotography/iStockphoto, 27; pingebat/Shutterstock.com, 28-29

ISBN
978-1-63235-563-8 (hardcover)
978-1-63235-617-8 (paperback)
978-1-63235-679-6 (hosted ebook)

Library of Congress Control Number: 2018937843

Printed in the United States of America
Mankato, MN
June, 2018

About the Cover
Japanese snow monkeys stay warm in
the hot springs near Nagano, Japan.

Access free, up-to-date content on this topic plus a full digital version of this book. Scan the QR code on page 31 or use your school's login at 12StoryLibrary.com.

Table of Contents

Fairy Penguins Parade Each Evening in Australia

It's a little before sunset on Phillip Island, Australia. Hundreds of people gather on stands on the boardwalk. They keep watch on the beach. Darkness falls. Everyone keeps their eyes on the sea. Suddenly the crowd gasps. Someone yells, "Look! Over there!"

One by one, and then in swarms, penguins pop out of the sea. They hurry across the beach and make their way to their burrows. Some penguins parade single file. Others waddle together in packs.

The penguins on parade are little blue penguins. Australians call them fairy penguins. At only 13 to 15 inches (36 to 42 cm) tall, they are the smallest penguins

Fairy penguins stay in groups of two to ten for safety.

32,000
Little blue penguins living on Phillip Island.

- Little blue penguins go fishing an hour or two before sunrise each day.
- They return to land shortly after sunset.
- Hundreds of people watch the penguins return to shore each night.

PENGUIN JUMPERS

Penguin jumpers are not jumping penguins. They are penguin sweaters. Oil the size of a thumbnail can kill a little penguin. If oil gets on their feathers, they can swallow it during preening. Sweaters are placed on penguins caught in an oil spill. This keeps the penguins from preening until they can be cleaned.

in the world. The parade begins each evening, when the penguins arrive home from a day of fishing. They wait until just after sunset. The penguins hope to escape the notice of hungry birds such as Pacific gulls and sea eagles.

Within an hour, most of the 2,000 penguins living nearby have returned to their burrows. They settle in for the night. One or two hours before sunrise, they wake. They swim out to sea to fish again.

Sweaters keep the penguins from preening until oil can be cleaned from their feathers.

Endangered Animals Gather in the Okavango Delta

The Okavango Delta is a huge oasis in the Kalahari Desert. Located in the northern part of Botswana, it is home to some of the most endangered mammals in the world. Black and white rhinos, cheetahs, lions, and African wild dogs all live there. Some animals live in the delta year-round. Others follow the water.

Summer in the delta begins in October. The waters recede as the air heats up. Summer rains start to fall in November. This brings only temporary relief to the area. The delta waters do not rise. The rains stop falling in April or May. The land begins to dry. Upstream, the river starts flooding. The water flows, making its way to the delta

130
Mammal species found in the Okavango Delta.

- The Okavango Delta collects water from the Okavango River.
- The height of the water in the delta varies throughout the year.
- The delta is home to a wide variety of animals, plants, and birds.

Travel in a mokoro in the Okavango Delta.

A SPECIAL DELTA

Most river deltas are fan-like areas at the end of a river. Water collects in the delta before flowing into the sea. The Okavango Delta is different. It is an inland delta. Its water filters down into the Kalahari Desert sands.

at the end of its winter season. The delta waters peak between July and September.

This is a good time to see large herds of African elephant,

buffalo, and zebra. They drink, splash, and play in the Okavango Delta's clear water. Islands dot the flooded area. Some are made from stands of trees. Some are termite mounds sticking up above the surface.

Visitors explore the area by boat. The adventurous ones travel in a local dugout canoe called a mokoro. Hippos, crocodiles, and tiny reed frogs live in and around the water. Other animals and birds come to drink or fish.

The Okavango is home to many elephants.

Unique Animals Live on the Galápagos Islands

The Galápagos Islands are home to many plants and animals that are found nowhere else on Earth. This archipelago of 19 islands is located 620 miles (1,000 km) off the coast of Ecuador. The volcanic islands are harsh and isolated.

On land, visitors may see giant tortoises, marine iguanas, and sea lions. Resident birds include Galápagos penguins, blue-footed

100

Maximum number of people allowed on a Galápagos tour boat.

- The Galápagos Islands are an archipelago off the coast of Ecuador.
- Many unique animals live in and around the Galápagos.
- Travel to the Galápagos is limited to protect the wildlife.

Small boats bring visitors close to the wildlife.

SLOW GIANTS

The giant Galápagos tortoise is the world's largest tortoise. They measure up to 5 feet (1.5 m) long. They can weigh as much as 550 pounds (249 kg). They live to be over 100 years old. They live a lazy life, napping almost 16 hours a day. This slow life allows them to survive up to a year without eating or drinking.

boobies, flightless cormorants, and waved albatross.

The Galápagos waters hold more treasure. They host many kinds of sharks. These include hammerhead, whale, and white-tipped reef sharks. Divers may see stingrays, spotted

eagle rays, and manta rays. Green sea turtles are also a common sight underwater.

People cannot stay on most of the islands. They can only access them on small boat tours. Tour operators must be registered with the government. These restrictions are efforts to protect the Galápagos land and wildlife.

Since access is restricted, travel to the Galápagos requires lots of planning. There is no bad time to go. Different animals are present and active at different times during the year. People usually plan their trips around the animals they want to see.

The oldest Galápagos tortoise on record lived to be 152 years old.

4

People Swim with Whale Sharks in the Indian Ocean

South Ari Atoll in the Maldives offers an opportunity most other places can't. Here, people can swim with a fish about the size of a school bus. Whale sharks may be the largest fish on Earth, but they are gentle giants.

Whale sharks have huge mouths, up to 4 or 5 feet (1.2–1.5 m) across. They can't swallow a human, though. Their throats are tiny, about the size of a quarter. They also lack the scary teeth people associate with sharks. Whale shark teeth are numerous but tiny.

Whale sharks often feed close to the surface.

A whale shark doesn't chomp its prey. It's a filter feeder. It fills its mouth with food like zooplankton and fish eggs. Water moves out through its gills. Food gathers in the back of its mouth. Once it has a ball of food, the shark gulps it down. It spits out anything too big to swallow.

Whale sharks live in warm seas around the world. In most places, they swim deep. In the Maldives, they stay closer to the surface. Whale sharks live in the Maldives year-round. That makes this Indian Ocean archipelago an excellent place to see them and swim with them.

After swimming with sharks, people can have dinner below them. The Maldives is home to the world's first undersea restaurant, Ithaa. Diners eat 16 feet (5 m) below the Indian Ocean. The glass-domed ceiling provides unique views of marine life. Lucky eaters may see a whale shark swim by.

300
Rows of tiny teeth in a whale shark's jaw.

- Whale sharks are gentle giants.
- They live around the world in warm waters.
- People can see whale sharks year-round in the Maldives.

THINK ABOUT IT

Plastics in the ocean can harm whale sharks. What can you do to keep plastics from getting in the ocean?

5

Visitors Watch Sea Turtles Nest in Trinidad

In the dark of night, waves lap at the shore of a secluded beach. A large, lumbering body heaves itself out of the sea. A female leatherback sea turtle has come to nest. She digs a hole in the sand with her flippers. She lays about 80 eggs. She gently covers her nest with sand. Then she follows the moon's light back to the sea. Two months later, the eggs hatch. The baby turtles find their way to the sea on their own.

In Trinidad, sea turtles nest from March to September. If a turtle is lucky, she nests on Matura Beach. Turtle nests there are unlikely to be disturbed. Matura sits on the island's eastern shore. Up to 150 turtles may nest there at one time. But no more than 100 people are allowed on the beach at one time. Visitors have a great view without disturbing the turtles.

Some visitors do more than watch. They team up with scientists from Earthwatch Institute. They patrol the beach at night. When a

People can help measure turtles for research.

nesting turtle arrives, the team gets to work. They measure the turtle. They note the turtle's tag. If there is none, they add one to a flipper. The team notes the conditions around the turtle. What is the weather like? How many people are on the beach?

The team may also dig up old nests. They try to determine how many of the eggs hatched. They look at how many nests washed out to sea. All this data helps scientists keep track of and learn about the turtles. This leads to efforts that help the turtles.

Baby turtles make their way to the sea on their own.

880
Weight of average leatherback turtle in pounds (400 kg).

- Leatherback sea turtles nest on Matura Beach from March to September.
- Female turtles come ashore to lay their eggs.
- Volunteers monitor the nesting activities.

6

Stingrays Gather in Grand Cayman

Most public aquariums have tanks where visitors can touch a small stingray. For those who want to touch a ray in the wild, Stingray City is the place to go.

Stingray City is not an actual city. It is a sandbar in the North Sound of Grand Cayman. Up to 50 stingrays call this place home. They swarm around visitors who wade in the warm Caribbean Sea. The stingrays know that the people bring food.

The shallow sandbar and clear waters allow visitors to get close.

Stingrays feel safe knowing they'll receive food.

The stingrays moved in during the 1980s. Local fishermen grew tired of bugs bothering them as they cleaned their catch on land. They began cleaning their catch in the bug-free North Sound. The fishermen threw their fish waste into the water. The stingrays took advantage of the free meals. Soon the stingrays flocked to the sound of a boat engine. Now the stingrays are fed by tourists, not fishermen.

Stingrays get their name from their barbed tails. When threatened, stingrays swing their tails. A hit from a stingray tail can hurt. Visitors usually have nothing to fear from gentle stingrays.

10
Number of stingray pups that may be born in one litter.

- Stingrays gather for free food in Stingray City in Grand Cayman.
- The practice started in the 1980s.
- Stingrays are gentle, but can inflict hurt when threatened.

THINK ABOUT IT

Legend says kissing a stingray brings seven years of good luck. Many tour operators scoop wild stingrays out of the sea for visitors to kiss. Do you think this is a good practice? Why or why not?

7

Monarchs Winter in the Mexican Mountains

Each autumn, millions of butterflies fly to the mountains of Angangueo, Mexico. Their large numbers darken the sky like clouds. Their beating wings sound like light rain falling. They land in trees by the thousands. Branches bend under their weight.

Monarch butterflies from east of the Rocky Mountains winter in the Mexican mountains. They travel up to 3,000 miles (4,828 km) to get there. This winter home has temperatures that range from 32 to 50 degrees Fahrenheit (0–10°C). Monarchs need to be cool but not cold to survive.

The first monarchs arrive in Mexico in November. They settle on oyamel fir trees. Butterflies continue to arrive over the next month or two. They huddle together on tree trunks and branches to keep warm. They pack in tightly. Each tree becomes a mass of black and orange.

Monarchs huddle together to stay warm.

THE SUPER GENERATION

The same butterflies that flew to Mexico begin the trip back north. These monarchs are part of the super generation. Their parents and children complete their life cycle in four weeks. The super generation lives for months and travels thousands of miles. It takes three or four generations to complete the journey to Canada.

Monarchs migrate up to 3,000 miles.

In winter, the butterflies spend much of their time sleeping. Temperatures warm in February and March. The monarchs wake. This is the best time to see them. They flutter about. They sun themselves. They drink from ponds and puddles. They breed and begin their journey home. Monarchs are the only butterfly to make this two-way migration.

265
Longest recorded one-day flight by a monarch, in miles (426 km).

- Millions of monarch butterflies travel to Mexico every autumn.
- Monarchs spend their winter sleeping in the Sierra Madre mountains.
- The monarchs start their return trip north in March.

Goats Climb Trees in Morocco

Southwestern Morocco has a desert climate. Trees grow sparsely there. One tree, the argan, dominates the landscape near the city of Essaouira. It looks short and scraggly. Its bark is rough and thorny. Its roots grow deep into the ground. These roots protect the area from erosion. They keep the desert from creeping in. This scruffy but important tree is the site of an animal adventure.

Fruit grows on the argan trees. In summer, the fruit ripens. Local farmers then release their goats. These goats love argan fruit so much they'll climb the trees to get it. They'll even climb to the top of a 30-foot (9-m) tree. A dozen goats may gather in one tree to have a feast.

The argan fruit is a small, yellow fruit with a tough skin. Each fruit holds up to three almond-shaped nuts within

Goats eat the argan fruit for over six hours every day.

it. These nuts are the source of argan oil. This oil is a popular ingredient in beauty products.

Legend says the goats poop out the argan nuts, which are then harvested by the locals. The local people do harvest argan nuts. But scientists determined the nuts come from goat spit, not goat poo. By autumn, the goats have eaten all the argan fruit. They then move on to feast on the argan tree leaves. This can harm the trees.

Goats spit out the argan nuts.

450
Lifespan of an argan tree in years.

- Argan trees are important to southwestern Morocco.
- Argan trees grow a small fruit containing argan nuts.
- Argan oil is used in beauty products.
- Goats climb the trees to eat the fruit.

Bats Swarm Each Evening in New Mexico

Every summer evening, visitors to Carlsbad Caverns National Park gather in an outdoor amphitheater. They sit on stone benches facing the mouth of a cave. Then they wait for the bat show to start.

The bats leave the cave each evening in a swarm. They spiral out of the cave, thousands at a time. Visitors can smell the bats as they fly overhead. The beating of their wings provides a soundtrack to the night. This show can last up to three hours.

The bats spend the night eating flying insects. They return to their roosts before dawn. Their return is just as exciting as their flight out. From hundreds of feet in the air, the bats dive into the cave.

The Carlsbad caves are the summer home to 300,000–400,000

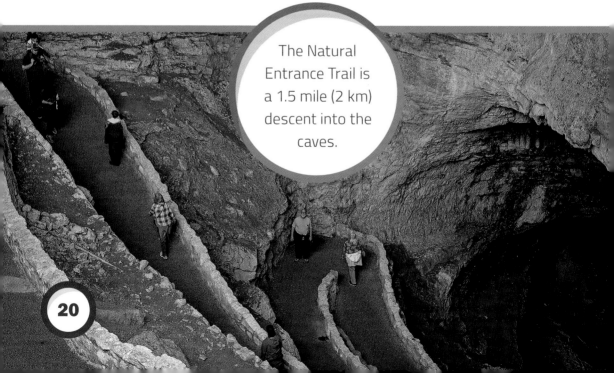

The Natural Entrance Trail is a 1.5 mile (2 km) descent into the caves.

Bats consume between 200 and 600 insects a night.

Brazilian free-tailed bats. They've come to New Mexico to have their babies. In August and September, the bat pups join their parents on their nightly trips. This is when the bat show is the most impressive.

25

Maximum flight speed of a Brazilian free-tailed bat, in mph (40 km/h).

- Brazilian free-tailed bats live in Carlsbad Caverns in the summer months.
- Every night, they leave the cave in a swarm to find food.
- Their pups join them in August.

BATS GALORE

Carlsbad Caverns hosts 17 different species of bats. Only three of those live in the caves. The Brazilian free-tailed bats provide the nightly show. The other cave-dwelling bats usually leave the cave later in the evening. The remaining bats roost in trees and cracks in rocks.

10

Monkeys Soak in Hot Springs in Japan

Snow monkey is another name for the Japanese macaque. Snow monkeys live in the forests of Japan. The only primates that live further north on Earth are humans. Unlike humans, snow monkeys live outside all winter.

Snow monkeys are adapted for the cold. Their thick fur coats help keep them warm in temperatures as low as minus 5 degrees Fahrenheit

(-15°C). Their stumpy tails are unlikely to get frostbite. And they're smart. When temperatures drop, they take a dip in a hot spring.

People travel long distances to get a glimpse of snow monkeys lounging in hot springs. One place to see this is near Nagano, a city on Japan's main island. There is a park called Jigokudani Yaen-Koen, which means Paradise of the Monkeys. It is also

The hot springs can reach 109° F (43°C) or higher.

Adult macaques weigh about 33 pounds (15 kg) and stand about 2 feet (60 cm) tall.

known as Wild Snow Monkey Park because the monkeys come and go as they please.

The snow monkeys live in the forests around Jigokudani. They come to the park to find food and bathe in the hot springs. Visitors who want to see the monkeys bathing should come in the winter, when the air is cold. Snow monkeys only bathe to stay warm. They don't like to get in the water during warm seasons.

ROCK OUT

What do snow monkeys do when they're not foraging or bathing? They might play with rocks. Japanese macaques are sometimes seen stacking rocks and knocking them down again. Others cuddle their rocks. The monkeys usually play with rocks alone. Seeing others playing with rocks makes them want to play,

3.5
Length in inches (9 cm) of a snow monkey's tail.

- Snow monkeys live the furthest north of any nonhuman primate.
- They live in the forests of Japan.
- When winter gets frigid, they bathe in hot springs.
- One of the best places to see the monkeys is near Nagano.

White Horses Run Wild in France

The Camargue region is often called the Wild West of France. There, the cowboys are called *gardians.* They ride small white horses and herd black bulls. The Camargue sits in the delta of the Rhone River. It is a large patchwork of wetlands, grasslands, and woods. It is known for its diverse wildlife population.

Bird watchers come to see the hundreds of bird species there. Most people look forward to seeing the flocks of pink flamingos. The Camargue birds are more white than pink, though.

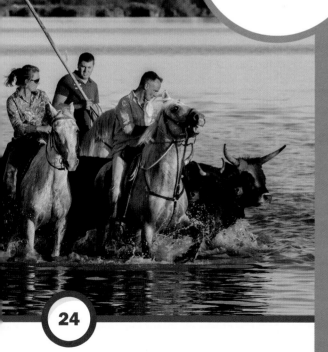

Gardians on Camargue horses herd a bull.

1978
The year Camargue horses were recognized as a unique breed.

- The Camargue is a marshy area in the Rhone delta.
- Many different species of animals live there.
- The white horses are the most famous residents.
- Visitors often tour the Camargue on horseback.

Horse riding is one of the popular ways to discover Camargue National Park.

The region's most famous animals trot along on four legs. They swim in the sea. They splash through the marshes. They are the white Camargue horses. These horses are not just pretty. They are small, rugged, and level-headed. They are equally sure-footed on the beach, in the marshes, and on pavement. This makes them excellent for riding and herding.

One of the best ways to see the Camargue is on the back of one of their horses. The calm horses allow even beginners to ride.

CHANGING COLORS

Visitors may be surprised to see brown horses frolicking along with the white. These dark horses are not different breeds. They are young Camargue horses. The horses are born with brown or black coats. Their coats turn white when they are four or five years old.

25

Big Bears Gather to Fish in Alaska

People watch a brown bear dig for clams.

Some of the largest bears in the world live in Alaska. Each summer, tourists travel to the Kodiak Archipelago hoping to see them.

Kodiak bears are a type of brown bear. Brown bears made their way from the mainland to Kodiak 12,000 years ago. Rising seas stranded these bears on Kodiak. Isolated, they evolved into a new subspecies. Kodiak bears grew larger than mainland bears. A male Kodiak bear weighs up to 1,400 pounds (635 kg). Standing on its hind legs, it can measure 10 feet (3 m) tall. Like most bears, Kodiaks stay in their dens all winter. They enter as early as October. They come out as late as June. The best chance to see a Kodiak bear comes in July, August, and September.

Kodiak bears spend their days finding food. They love salmon and

Fish make up the majority of the Kodiak's diet.

spend much time fishing in streams. In July, the bears add berries to their diet. They also eat deer, elk, and cattle. Kodiak bears like to be alone. They tolerate groups to get their favorite foods. Those who really want to see Kodiak bears travel with a guide.

3,500
Number of Kodiak bears on the Archipelago as of 2016.

- Kodiak bears are found only on the Kodiak Archipelago.
- They spend most of their time searching for food.
- To see Kodiak bears, travel with a guide in the late summer months.

THINK ABOUT IT

What is the largest bear in the world? It's either a male polar bear or a male Kodiak bear. Polar bears weigh 900–1,500 pounds (408–608 kg). Kodiak bears weigh 600–1,400 pounds (272–635 kg). Polar bears stand 8 to 8.4 feet (2.4 to 2.6 m) tall. Kodiak bears stand 7 to 10 feet (2.1 to 3.1 m) tall. So which is larger?

Where in the World?

Big bears forage for fish and berries in Kodiak, Alaska.

Brazilian free-tailed bats put on a show each evening as they exit their roosts in Carlsbad Caverns National Park, New Mexico.

Many monarch butterflies spend their winters in Angangueo, Mexico.

Stingrays gather around tourists wading in the Caribbean waters of Stingray City, Grand Cayman.

Many animals living on the Galápagos Islands in Ecuador are not found anywhere else on Earth.

Volunteer tourists help collect data on leatherback sea turtles at Matura Beach, Trinidad.

CANADA

UNITED STATES

MEXICO

VENEZUELA

COLOMBIA

BRAZIL

PERU

BOLIVIA

ARGENTINA

Greenland (DENMARK)

ICELAND

SPAIN

MAURITANIA

MALI

UNITED STATES

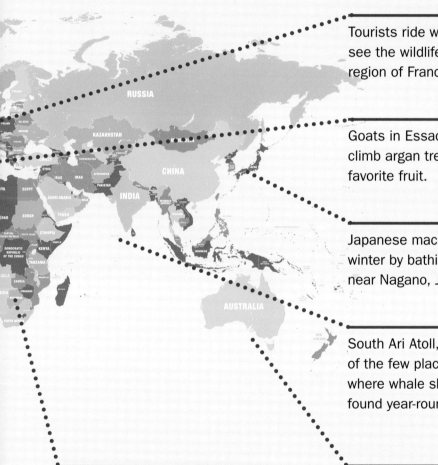

Tourists ride white horses to see the wildlife in the Camargue region of France.

Goats in Essaouira, Morocco, climb argan trees to eat their favorite fruit.

Japanese macaque stay warm in winter by bathing in hot springs near Nagano, Japan.

South Ari Atoll, Maldives, is one of the few places in the world where whale sharks can be found year-round.

The Okavango Delta in Botswana is home to some of the most endangered animals in the world.

Fairy penguins on Phillip Island, Australia, parade across the beach each evening when they return from fishing in the sea.

Glossary

amphitheater
A theater, often with no roof, where seats are curved around in an oval or circle.

archipelago
A stretch of water that has many islands.

barb
A sharp point that sticks out and in the opposite direction of the main point.

diverse
Made up of lots of different kinds or types.

erosion
The wearing away of dirt and sand by wind and water.

evolve
To change little by little over time into a different state or version.

frostbite
An injury to the body caused by exposure to extreme cold.

migration
The act of moving from one location to another, usually on a regular schedule, to feed or breed.

oasis
A green spot in the desert where water is found.

preen
To clean and arrange feathers using a beak.

recede
To move away or dry up, as in flood waters.

zooplankton
Tiny animals drifting in the ocean.

For More Information

Books

Cerullo, Mary M. *Seeking Giant Sharks (Shark Expedition)*. North Mankato, MN: Compass Point Books, 2014.

Stine, Megan. *Where Are the Galapagos Islands?* New York: Grosset & Dunlap, 2017.

Pringle, Laurence. *Penguins!: Strange and Wonderful.* Honesdale, PA: Boyds Mills Press, 2013.

Visit 12StoryLibrary.com

Scan the code or use your school's login at **12StoryLibrary.com** for recent updates about this topic and a full digital version of this book. Enjoy free access to:

- Digital ebook
- Breaking news updates
- Live content feeds
- Videos, interactive maps, and graphics
- Additional web resources

Note to educators: Visit 12StoryLibrary.com/register to sign up for free premium website access. Enjoy live content plus a full digital version of every 12-Story Library book you own for every student at your school.

31

Index

About the Author

Janet Slingerland was an engineer before she started writing books. She lives in New Jersey with her husband, three children, and a dog. She loves going on adventures with her family.